# Top Cat

# Top Cat

SCRITCH
SCRATCH

## Lois Ehlert

SCHOLASTIC INC.
New York  Toronto  London  Auckland  Sydney
Mexico City  New Delhi  Hong Kong

O-KA-LEE
O-KA-LEE

I'm top cat.
Pet me, I'll purr.

I guard this place
in my coat of fur.

PURR
URR
PURR
URR

Boring job! Never see a
Nothing much happens
in this dull house.

mouse.

Who let you in?
One cat's
enough.

ME-OW
SCRATCH
SCRATCH
SCRATCH
ME-OW

SNIFF
SNIFF

I don't want to
share my stuff.

IMAN

CIET

SWISH
SWISH

SWISH
SWISH

Go away, cat!

GRRRR
HISS
HISS

You've
invaded
my space.

SWISH
SWISH

CHEEP
CHEEP
CHEEP

GRRRR
HISS
HISS

And I don't like your cute little face.

SWISH
SWISH

I'll fight you and bite
you behind the ear.
Get the message?
I'm boss
around here.

Well, you're here
to stay.
I can see that.

SCRATCH
SCRATCH

Guess I'm
stuck with you,
striped cat.

SWISH

JINGLE JINGLE

THUNK

But there's more to do than eat and sleep.

JINGLE
JINGLE

WHIZ

Keep your
green eyes
open.
Watch me
leap!

Bounce on the couch. Leave lots of hair.

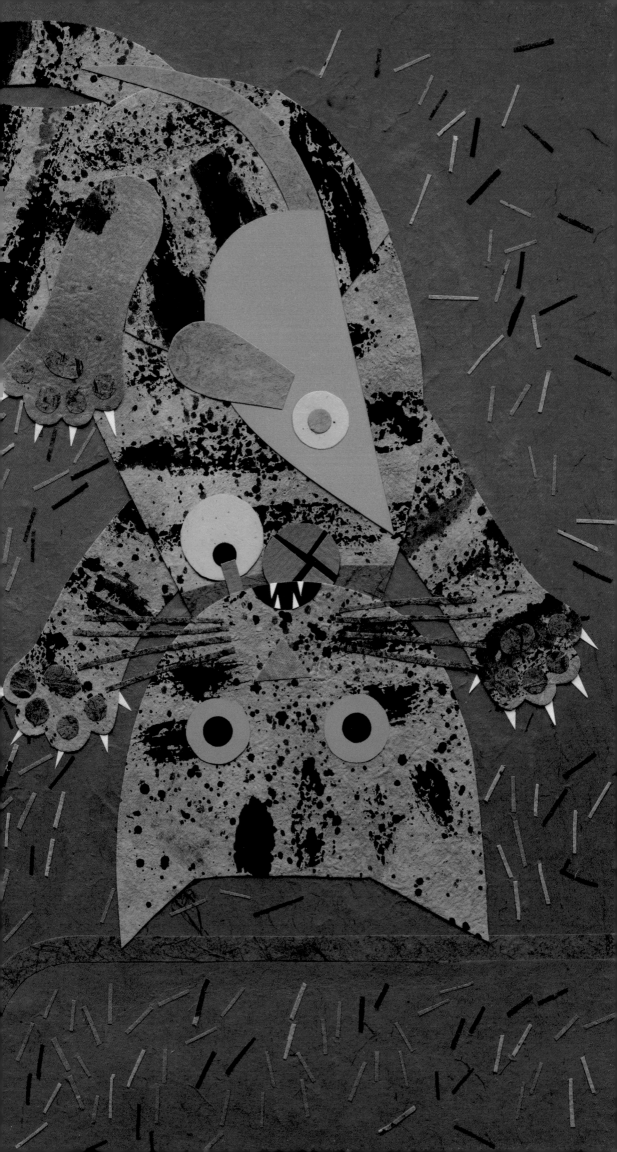

# Eat leaves till the plants are bare.

CHOMP

CHOMP

Drink from the sink wher

DRIP

company's there.

Dance on the table with the silverware.

JINGLE JINGLE

CLINK CLANK

Door's
left open?
Go get
some
fresh air.

JINGLE
JINGLE

JINGLE
JINGLE

WHOOSH

Test your claws.
Give birds a good scare.

JINGLE
JINGLE

Time
to eat!
You'd
better
decide.

Will you come in
or stay outside?

WHAT
CHEER
WIT
WIT
WIT

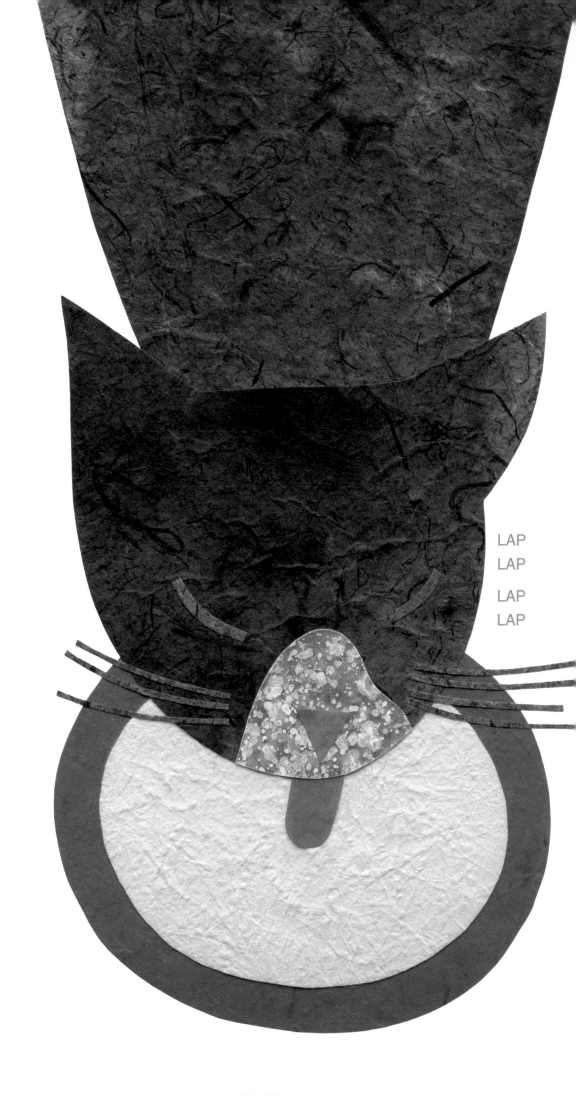

LAP
LAP

LAP
LAP

Welcome back!
Let's drink milk
in our furs.
No hisses,
no scratches,
no bites.

Just
purrs.

LIP
LIP
LIP
LIP

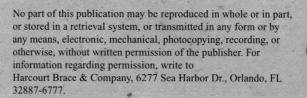

# For Shirley and Don

ISBN 0-439-08671-X

Published by Scholastic Inc., 555 Broadway,
New York, NY 10012, by arrangement with
Harcourt Brace & Company.

12 11 10 9 8 7 6 5 4 3 2          9/9 0 1 2 3 4/0

Printed in the U.S.A.                              08

First Scholastic printing, September 1999

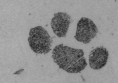

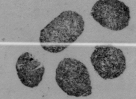